MERMAID DAYS™

The Sea Monster

Read more MERMAID DAYS books!

MERMAID DAYS

The Sea Monster

WRITTEN BY
Kyle Lukoff

ART BY
Kat Uno

ACORN™
SCHOLASTIC INC.

To Alix, who inspired Mr. Burbles.
—**KL**

To my family, thank you for giving me the motivation to work towards my dreams.
—**KU**

Text copyright © 2022 by Kyle Lukoff.
Illustrations copyright © 2022 by Kat Uno.

Library of Congress Cataloging-in-Publication Data Available

Names: Lukoff, Kyle, author. | Uno, Kat, illustrator.
Title: The sea monster / by Kyle Lukoff ; illustrated by Kat Uno.
Description: First edition. | New York : Acorn/Scholastic Inc., 2022. |
Series: Mermaid days ; 2 | Audience: Ages 5–7. | Audience: Grades K–1. |
Summary: Vera the mermaid and her half-octopus friend Beaker meet a friendly kraken on a field trip.
Identifiers: LCCN 2021045095 | ISBN 9781338794656 (paperback) | ISBN 9781338794687 (hardcover)
Subjects: LCSH: Mermaids—Juvenile fiction. | Kraken—Juvenile fiction. | Marine animals—Juvenile fiction. | CYAC: Mermaids—Fiction. | Kraken—Fiction. | Marine animals—Fiction. | LCGFT: Picture books.
Classification: LCC PZ7.1.L8456 Se 2022 | DDC [E]—dc23
LC record available at https://lccn.loc.gov/2021045095

10 9 8 7 6 5 4 3 2 1   22 23 24 25 26

Printed in China   62
First edition, September 2022
Edited by Rachel Matson
Designed by Jaime Lucero

TABLE OF CONTENTS

On the Shore 1

The Sea Monster 18

The Visitor 40

WHO LIVES IN TIDAL GROVE?

Vera

Beaker

Beaker's Legs

Cuttle

Mr. Burbles

Frond

Ms. Dorsal

ON THE SHORE

DID YOU KNOW?

Tide pools are shallow pools of seawater. You can find them where the ocean meets the land!

Tide pools are home to all sorts of plants and animals.

LIBRARIAN

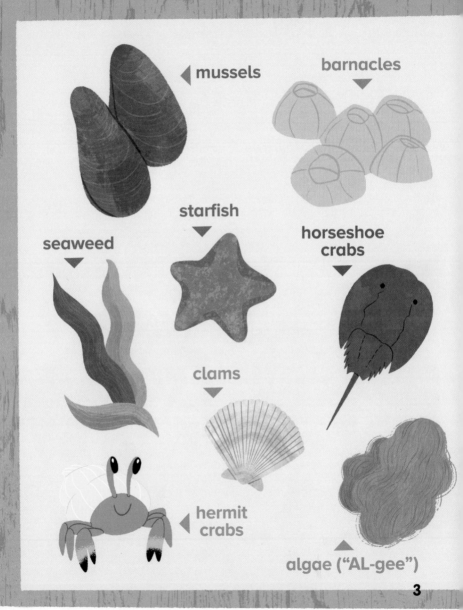

mussels

barnacles

starfish

seaweed

horseshoe crabs

clams

hermit crabs

algae ("AL-gee")

3

I love field trips with Ms. Dorsal!

Me too!

I've never been to the tide pools before. I want to play with a hermit crab.

I want to pet a starfish!

4

The animals might be scared of you. Try to be quiet and still. Then see what happens.

13

14

That's okay. The dragonflies were making me itchy. Let's go look at that starfish!

THE SEA MONSTER

I loved going to the tide pools.

I wanted to see clams at the tide pools. But they must have been hiding in the sand.

I bet clams think we look huge.

Have you ever heard of a kraken?

No. What's a kraken?

23

A kraken is a sea monster.
They might look like giant squids.
But <u>extra</u> giant.

Do they squirt
clouds of ink like
normal squids?

They probably
squirt <u>giant</u>
clouds of ink!

Cuttle! I'll get you!

pop!

Frond, where are you?

Right behind you!
Can I grab your tail?

Yes. Don't
get lost.

Oops!

You dropped it!

It was slippery.

Where did the human thing go?

It's sinking so fast!

I hope we can catch it.

34

THE VISITOR

Do you ever think about how big the ocean is?

Yes. I want to explore all of it!

Me too. There is so much to see!

43

There is a kraken outside!

ABOUT THE CREATORS

KYLE LUKOFF has never met a mermaid. He would very much like to be friends with an octopus! But he would rather climb trees than go to the beach, and he would rather write books for kids than learn how to scuba dive. He is a National Book Award finalist and the Newbery and Stonewall award—winning author of lots of books, including WHEN AIDAN BECAME A BROTHER and TOO BRIGHT TO SEE.

KAT UNO was born, raised, and currently resides in Hawaii. Living on an island surrounded by the beautiful Pacific Ocean has always provided much inspiration. Kat has loved being creative ever since she was little. She enjoys illustrating children's books, and mermaids are one of her favorite subjects to draw! She is also a proud mom of two voracious readers.

YOU CAN DRAW A KRAKEN!

1 Draw the outline of the head and eyes.

2 Draw the kraken's five tentacles.

3 Add the suckers on the tentacles!

4 Draw the kraken's face! Include the eyes, tusks, and smile.

5 Decorate your kraken with a pattern.

6 Color in your drawing!

WHAT'S YOUR STORY?

Vera and Beaker meet a kraken.
Imagine that **you** meet a friendly sea monster!
What does the monster look like?
What questions would you ask it?
Write and draw your story!